Pablo's Pet

Henry   Lily   Mei   Pablo   Padma

by **Sheri Tan**

illustrated by **Shirley Ng-Benitez**

Lee & Low Books Inc.   New York

For animal lovers everywhere —S.T.

To Harvey, Gretchen, Gabby, and Zsófi,
and to all the pets we love! —S.N-B.

LEE & LOW BOOKS Inc., 95 Madison Avenue, New York, NY 10016, leeandlow.com
Book design by Charice Silverman
Book production by The Kids at Our House
The illustrations are rendered in watercolor and altered digitally
Manufactured in China by Imago
Printed on paper from responsible sources
(hc) 10 9 8 7 6 5 4 3 2 1
(pb) 10 9 8 7 6 5 4 3 2 1
First Edition

Library of Congress Cataloging-in-Publication Data
Names: Tan, Sheri, author. | Ng-Benitez, Shirley, illustrator.
Title: Pablo's pet / by Sheri Tan; illustrated by Shirley Ng-Benitez.
Description: First edition. | New York: Lee & Low Books Inc., [2021]
Series: Dive into reading! ; 9 | Audience: Ages 4-7. | Audience: Grades K-1.
Summary: "Pablo learns to deal with the loss of his much-loved pet fish
with the help of his friends and family"— Provided by publisher.
Identifiers: LCCN 2020021732 | ISBN 9781643792071 (paperback)
ISBN 9781643792064 (hardcover) | ISBN 9781643794723 (ebook)
Subjects: CYAC: Fishes—Fiction. | Pets—Fiction. | Death—Fiction.
Grief—Fiction. | Hispanic Americans—Fiction.
Classification: LCC PZ7.T16125 Pab 2020 | DDC [E]—dc23
LC record available at https://lccn.loc.gov/2020021732

Contents

Story Time

Pablo was excited.
He could not wait to get home
to read to his pet fish, Ruby.

"I have a great book to read
to Ruby," Pablo told his friends
Lily, Padma, Mei, and Henry.
"It's about a fish who dreamed
he could fly."

When he got home,
Pablo went to see his pet.
Ruby was a beautiful
red fish.

"Hi, Ruby," said Pablo.
"I have a great book
to read to you.
It's about a fish who
dreamed he could fly."

Ruby usually swam toward Pablo
when he came by.
But this time she didn't swim
toward him.

"Are you tired, Ruby?"
asked Pablo.
"Okay, I will let you rest.
I can read to you tomorrow."

A Good Friend

The next morning,
Pablo woke up early.
He wanted to read the story
to Ruby before school.

He looked into Ruby's tank.
Ruby was not moving at all.

"Mom! Dad!" yelled Pablo.
"Something is wrong with Ruby!"
Pablo's mom and dad ran over.

"Oh, Pablo. I'm sorry, but Ruby has died," said Pablo's dad.

"What happened? I thought
I took good care of her,"
said Pablo. He started to cry.
"You did take good care
of her," said his mom.

"But sometimes it's just
a pet's time to go. Don't
worry. Ruby knew how much
you loved her."

At school Pablo had a hard time doing his work.

All he could think about was Ruby.

At recess everyone was playing,
except for Pablo.
"What's wrong, Pablo?" asked Lily.

"Ruby died," said Pablo.
He started to cry again.
Everyone hugged Pablo.
"I'm sorry," said Henry.
"She was a great pet."

"We have good memories of Ruby,"
said Padma.
"Yes, we do," said Pablo.

"Once my dad put a toy diver
in the tank. Ruby did not like it.
She pushed it over!"
Everyone laughed.
Suddenly, Pablo did not feel
so sad anymore.

"Ruby was a good friend,"
said Pablo.
"We should do something special
to remember her," said Lily.
"We could tell stories about
Ruby," said Padma.

"We could sing songs about Ruby,"
said Mei.
"What do you want to do, Pablo?"
asked Henry.

Pablo thought about Ruby.
Pablo thought about what to do
to remember her.

Then he knew what he wanted
to do for Ruby.
After school Pablo talked to his dad.
They went to a plant store together.

Goodbye

Later, Pablo's friends came over
to remember Ruby.
They made paper fish.

When they were done,
they marched out the door.
"We love you, Ruby," they sang.

Outside, Pablo, his family, and
his friends shared stories about Ruby.
Then Pablo and his dad buried her.
They planted a small tree nearby.
"The color of the leaves
remind me of Ruby," said Mei.

Pablo thought about his pet.
"Thank you for being my friend,"
he said.
"I will always remember you."

After his friends and family went
home, Pablo took out his library book.
He sat by the tree.

"There was once a fish who lived in a small pond," read Pablo. "And he dreamed about flying. . . ."

☆ **Activity** ☆

Pablo was very sad to lose Ruby. Have you ever had to say goodbye to a loved one or a pet that passed away? Write a letter to say goodbye. What would you tell that person or pet?

It can be hard to say goodbye to the people and pets we care about. What do you do to feel better when you are missing someone? Write a letter to Pablo sharing the things you do to feel better.

Do you have a pet? Draw a picture of your pet and write about a special memory that makes you smile.